I would like to introduce you to an old friend—
a character I created over a decade ago when I
myself lived in a cabin in a forest.

Whatever the season, Crinkleroot keeps his eyes
open and his nose poked out. He can find puzzles
hidden among the leaves and stories written in the
snow. There's nothing he'd like better than to
share them with you.

—Jim Arnosky
Ramtails, 1988

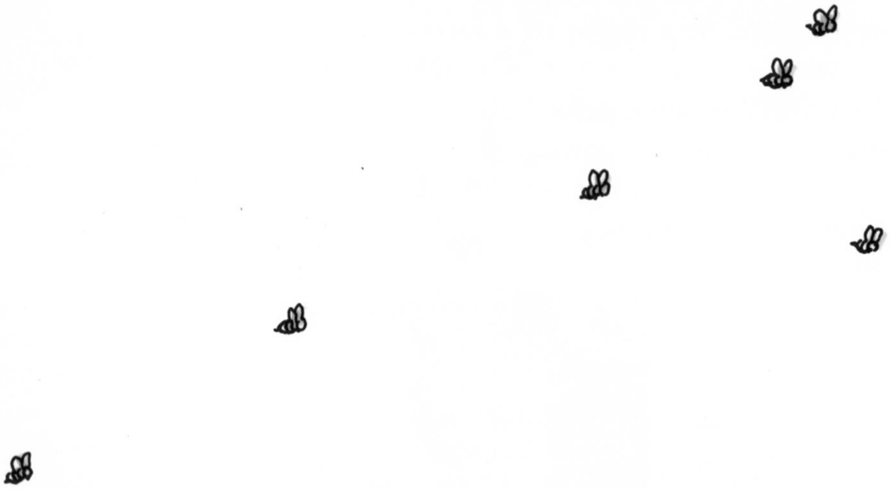

I WAS BORN IN A TREE AND RAISED BY BEES

JIM ARNOSKY

BRADBURY PRESS NEW YORK

I Was Born in a Tree and Raised by Bees was originally published in 1977
by G. P. Putnam's Sons in a 7 x 8½″ format, with black-and-white
and two-color illustrations throughout.
Text and illustrations copyright © 1977 by Jim Arnosky
Revised text and illustrations copyright © 1988 by Jim Arnosky

Bradbury Press
An Affiliate of Macmillan, Inc.
866 Third Avenue, New York, New York 10022
Collier Macmillan Canada, Inc.
Printed and bound in Japan
10 9 8 7 6 5 4 3 2 1

LIBRARY OF CONGRESS CATALOGING-IN-PUBLICATION DATA

Arnosky, Jim.
  I was born in a tree and raised by bees / by Jim Arnosky. — Rev.   p.
  Summary: Observations by the forest-dwelling Crinkleroot of the plants and
  animals that surround him.
  ISBN 0-02-705841-7 — USE THIS
  1. Natural history—Juvenile literature.   2. Forest ecology —
Juvenile literature.   [1. Forest animals.   2. Forest plants.
3. Nature study.]   I. Title.
QH48.A7 1988   508.315′2—dc19   88-6121   CIP   AC

FOR MY DEANNA

Hello. My name is Crinkleroot. I
was born in a tree and raised by bees. I
can whistle in a hundred languages and
speak caterpillar, turtle, and salamander, too!

I live in the deepest part of the forest, right under its tallest tree.

From my doorstep, I can feel the world slowly turning.

SPRING

It's spring, and everything is waking and coming alive. The bee tree near my woodpile is humming with worker bees, out searching for the first blossoms.

Inside, the queen bee is busy laying eggs. The queen is the mother of all the drones and workers that live in the hive. She is much larger than they are.

I'll climb up and see if I can pick her out for you.

See if you can find the queen bee among
all the bees on the honeycomb. Remember,
she is much bigger than the rest of
the bees in the hive.

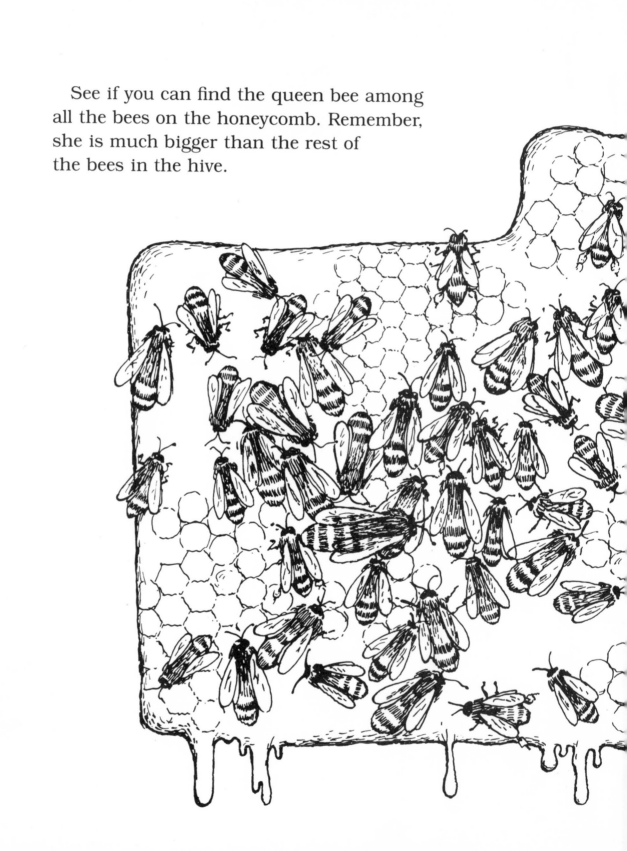

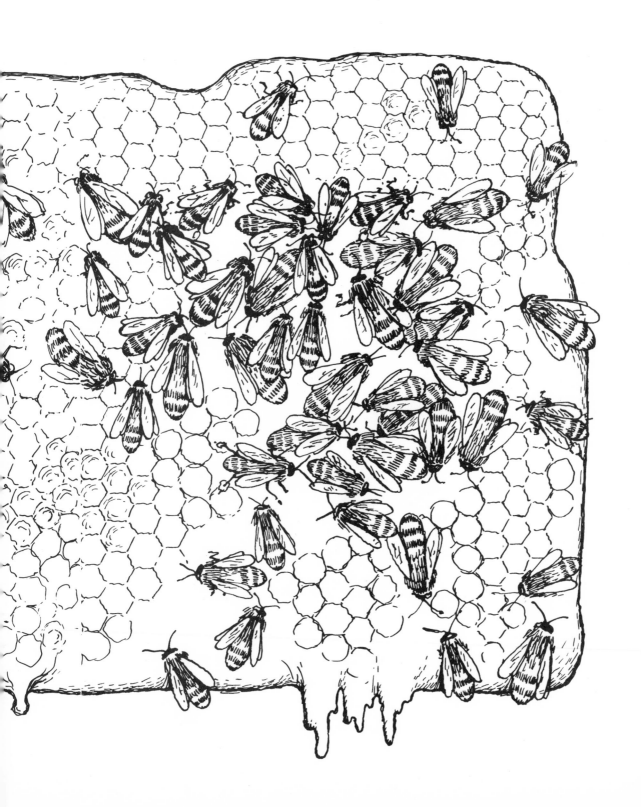

Look at these wildflowers poking up
through the leafy soil.

I like to remember where wildflowers grow
so I can stop and see them when they bloom.

I never pick any wildflowers.
I think they look pretty just where they are.
Plants and animals grow best in their
natural surroundings.

The moccasin orchid grows in bogs and
rocky woods where the soil is moist. Whoever
named this flower thought it looked
like an Indian's moccasin.

Trout lilies grow along the shady banks of streams.

Wild strawberries grow best
in sunny open thickets.

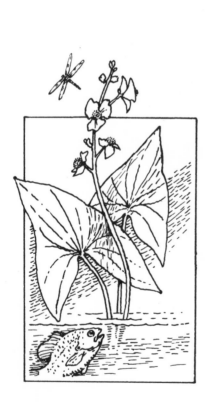

Arrowhead grows in shallow water.

I grow best wherever I can stretch out
my arms and breathe fresh clean air.

My! All this hunting for wildflowers has given me the munchies. Come inside while I pop some corn.

Popcorn is my favorite snack. I grow it in my garden. Do you know how popcorn grows? I'll show you, and then you can grow it, too.

This is a special place I like to visit. Sometimes I fish, and sometimes I just watch quietly. Often a deer will tiptoe down for a drink. On crisp autumn days I listen to the leaves falling on the water.

Tiny minnows swim in the stream. They sparkle in the ripples.

A kingfisher flies to the stream and
perches on an overhanging branch to watch for minnows.

This kingfisher is diving for supper.
How many minnows can you see?

SUMMER

Summer in the forest is a time of misty mornings and sunny afternoons. Turkeys perch in the treetops, and colorful snakes sun on hot dry rocks. An old woodsman told me he once pulled a rattlesnake out of his beard. It was more than ten feet long!

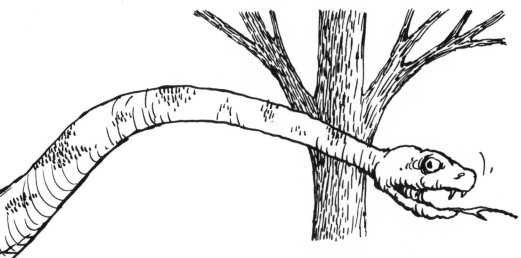

Toads are skillful hunters. They move
much more quickly than you think. If
you see a toad out in the open, it is
probably hunting. It sits as still as a
statue until an insect comes close to its
sticky tongue. Then, in a flash, it snatches
it up! Almost right away, the toad is just
like a statue again...waiting.

I've been watching this toad for a long
while now and I've seen him catch a
few bugs. How many times can you see it
snatch a meal?

It's such a nice night to stroll in the moonlight. If you are very quiet, you can see some of the shyest animals in the forest.

All the animals with me are nighttime
creatures. They sleep or hide all day,
waiting until it's dark to move about.

As summer is ending,
I like to pick leaves
from the trees.

Then I trace each leaf's shape on
a piece of paper.

Soon I have enough drawings to make
a leaf book. I tie the papers together
with yarn.

You can do the same thing. Then, when
you get to school in September, you and
your friends can look up the names of
all the trees.

AUTUMN

Leaves! Everywhere you look. Red leaves, yellow ones, gold or red, and nutty browns.

There is so much to see and smell and hear and feel in the autumn.

I like to sit quietly in the forest, close my eyes, and listen for sounds.

Be very still. Listen to the sounds.
How many do you know? How many
smells do you recognize?

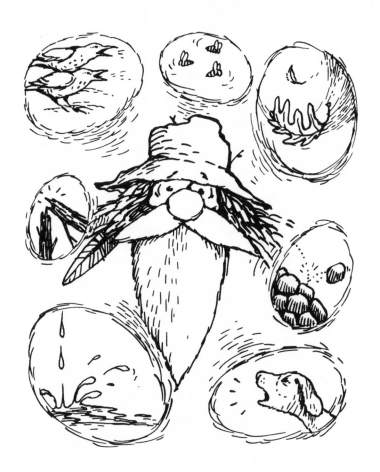

After awhile, you may be able to hear
sounds and smell smells most people
never even notice.

I was sitting, listening, when I heard
hoot...hoot coming from over here.

Owls are funny to watch. They cannot move their eyes around in their sockets like most creatures. They twist their heads into the oddest positions to see in different directions.

Once an owl I
was watching spread its
rounded wings and
glided silently down
after a snake. The snake
fought to escape, but the
owl was stronger and
won its meal.

Every creature depends on other creatures to survive. Owls eat snakes, snakes eat frogs, frogs eat dragonflies, dragonflies eat butterflies, and butterflies live on the sweet juices of flowers.

Some animals, like the opossum, eat many kinds of food. An opossum will eat anything from an earthworm to a robin's egg. Hidden here are different animals and plants that an opossum eats.

WINTER

As the weather gets colder, food in the forest is harder to find. Mice gnaw their way into my warm cabin. Raccoons make nightly visits to my garbage pile. Deer roam farther into the forest looking for food. I keep my bird feeders full of crunchy seeds and fatty suet.

Bird feeders are easy to build. My favorite is one I made from milk cartons. All the things you need to make one can be found around the house—three milk cartons, one long stick (about 18 inches), glue, twine, a pair of scissors, and some brown paint.

The only time of year I'm awake before the birds is the morning of winter's first snowfall. I like to see what wild creatures have been out and about during the night.

Animal tracks in the
snow always tell a story.
Follow these tracks
around my cabin, and
see what stories you can
read in the snow!

I snowshoed a bit farther into the forest this morning and came on a flock of wild turkeys. They looked so much like the forest itself I nearly missed them. How many turkeys do you see here?

Many animals roam about in the
cold weather, but others, like snakes
and woodchucks, sleep through the
winter in a warm comfortable place.
These animals are called hibernators.

There are animals hibernating in the frosty soil under my cabin.

The seasons are constantly
changing. Tonight I'm glad to have
my toasty wood stove.
But it won't be long
before I'll be smelling
spring in the wind and
the circle of the seasons
will be moving once
again.

Right now I'm going to
curl up by the fire and
do a bit of "hibernating"
myself.

Remember, there are pictures everywhere, puzzles hidden among the leaves and in the streams, and stories written on the snow. So keep your eyes open and your nose poked out, and someday you may be talking caterpillar, turtle, and salamander, too!

Crinkleroot

JIM ARNOSKY's first book for children, *I Was Born in a Tree and Raised by Bees*, reflects his admiration for such naturalists as John Muir and John Burroughs. Those who have enjoyed the author's work over the past decade will be delighted—but not surprised—to see his philosophy so fully expressed in this early work.

Jim Arnosky wrote and illustrated Crinkleroot's adventures while living at Hawk Mountain in Pennsylvania with his wife, Deanna, and their daughters, Michelle and Amber. Shortly after *I Was Born in a Tree and Raised by Bees* was first completed, the Arnoskys moved to an old farmhouse in Northern Vermont. There he wrote and illustrated *Drawing from Nature*, based largely on sketchbooks he'd begun at Hawk Mountain.

Published in 1982, *Drawing from Nature* won the Christopher Award for Nonfiction for All Ages and was named an ALA Notable Book. It marked the beginning of wide popular recognition of Jim Arnosky as an informed and enthusiastic guide to the natural world.

Jim Arnosky went on to write and illustrate such ALA Notable Books as *Drawing Life in Motion*; *Secrets of a Wildlife Watcher*; *Flies in the Water, Fish in the Air*; and *Sketching Outdoors in Spring*. In 1988, he brought the experience of looking at nature to television viewers by starring in a four-part nationwide PBS series based on *Drawing from Nature*.

Then he began thinking again about Crinkleroot and the fun of romping through the forest by his side.

1/12/91

D

N

C

MA